P9-BJE-631

IS ANYONE HUNGRY?

PETER PAVEY

Greenhouse Publications

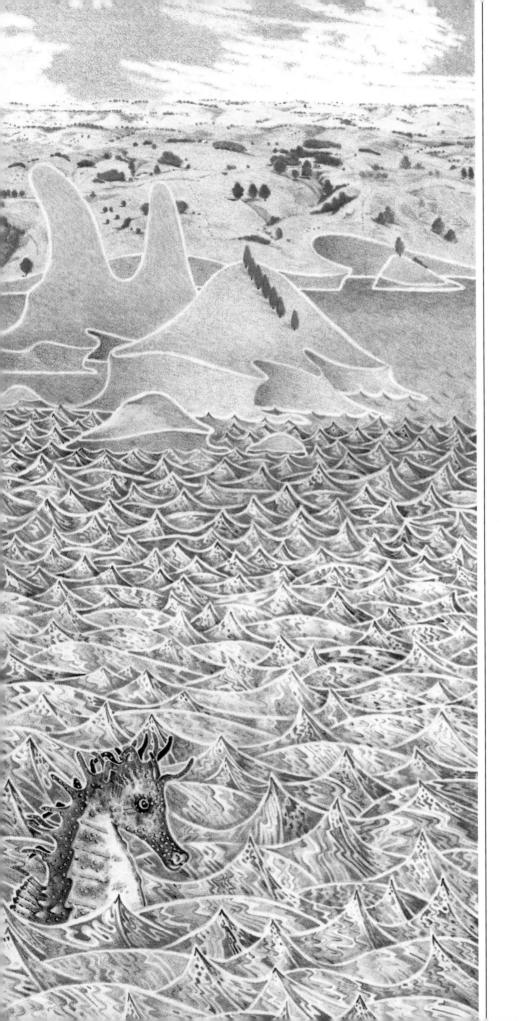

Alfred went to sea
to find the twittering grimbix

Alfred looked high
and he looked low
and he looked all around,
but nothing did he spy…

…except a giraffe.

Alfred asked the giraffe,
'Have you seen
the yellow-spotted,
twittering grimbix?'
'No', replied the giraffe,
'but I have seen
the purple, lumpy thumpet,
who is very angry
and very hungry too.'

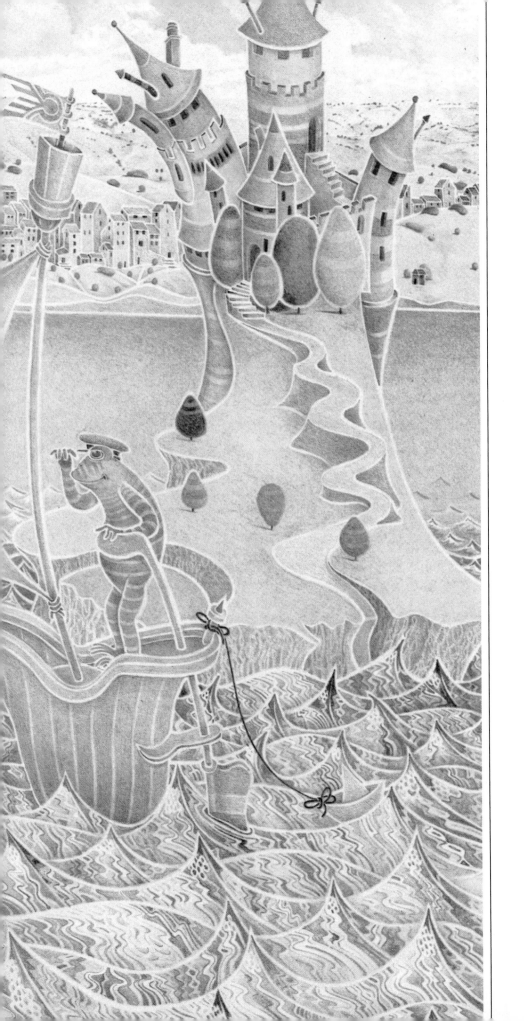

'Oh dear,' said Alfred
and sailed away,
looking high and looking low
and looking all around;
but nothing did he spy…

…except a rhinoceros.

Alfred asked the rhinoceros,
'Have you seen
the long-necked,
yellow-spotted,
twittering grimbix?'
'No,' grumbled
the rhinoceros
'but I have seen the green,
wide-eyed, fuzzy slobbit,
who is very, very angry
and very hungry too.'

'Oh dear,' said Alfred
and sailed away
looking here
and looking there
and looking all around;
but nothing did he spy…

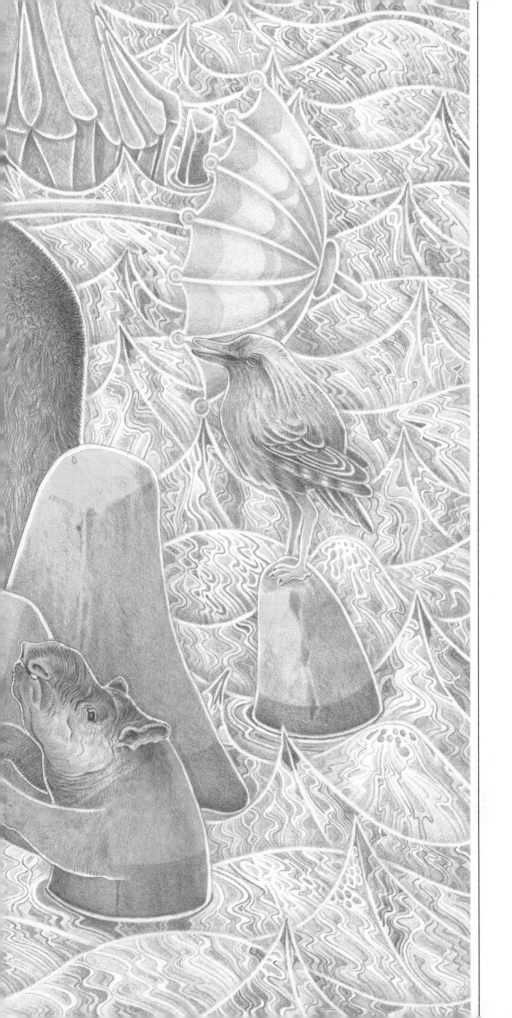

…except a bear.

Alfred asked the bear,
'Have you seen
the grinning, long-necked,
yellow-spotted,
twittering grimbix?'
'No,' replied the bear,
'but I have seen the red
flabby feegook,
who is very, very, very angry
and very hungry too.'

'Oh dear,' sighed Alfred
and sailed away,
looking up and looking down
and looking all around;
but nothing did he spy . . .

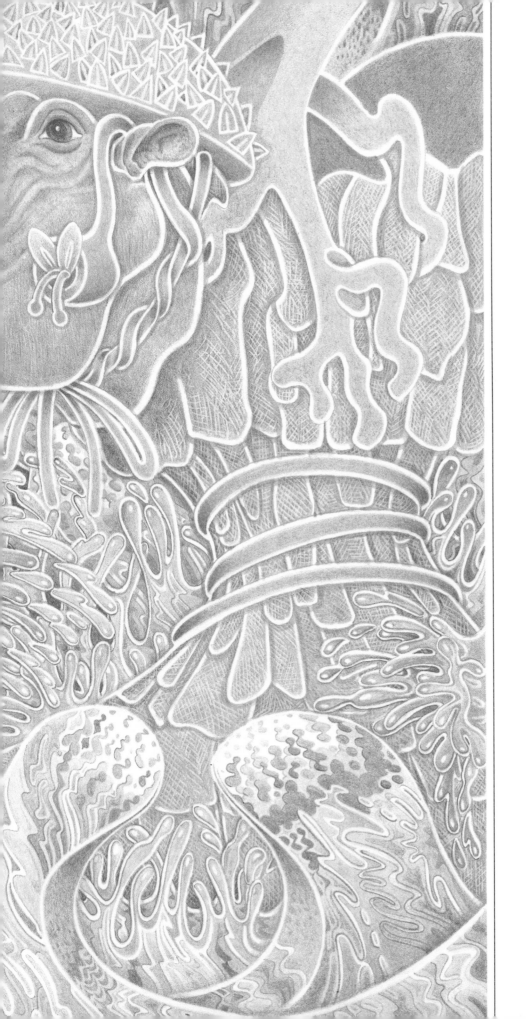

…except a hippopotamus.

Alfred asked the
hippopotamus,
'Have you seen
the three-tailed grinning,
long-necked,
yellow-spotted, twittering
grimbix?'
'No,' replied
the hippopotamus,
but I have seen the blue,
pesky bumberoo,
who is very angry,
very angry indeed,
and very hungry too.'

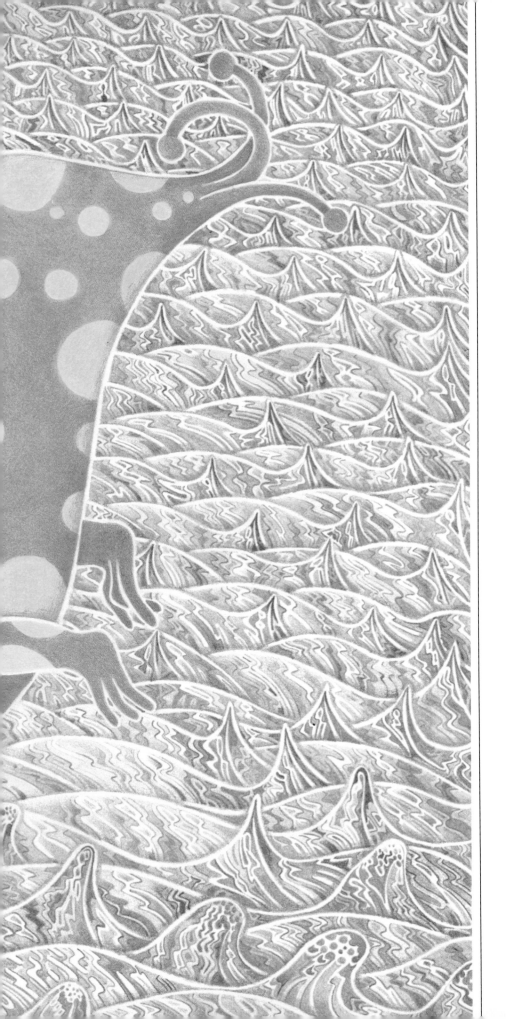

'Oh dear,' groaned Alfred
and he looked all around;
but nothing did he spy;
nothing at all.

Then Alfred realised
that he was hungry too.
He was about to eat his lunch,
when suddenly…

Eye to eye,
nose to nose,
he met
the three-tailed,
grinning,
long-necked,
yellow-spotted,
twittering grimbix!

'There you are!' gasped Alfred
and was about to ask
the grimbix if he was hungry,
when he heard
a very loud,
very fierce,
very deafening
and very frightening noise,
which shook the sea.

The purple, lumpy thumpet
trumpeted.
The green, fuzzy slobbit
slobbered.
The red, flabby feegook
frumbled
and the blue, pesky
bumberoo
burbled.

But Alfred just laughed,
as he reached for some apples
and said, 'Is anyone hungry?'

First published 1987 by
Greenhouse Publications Pty Ltd
385-387 Bridge Road
Richmond, 3121, Australia

© Peter Pavey, 1987

ISBN 0 86436 044 4
ISBN 0 86436 069X

Printed and bound in Hong Kong by
South China Printing Co.